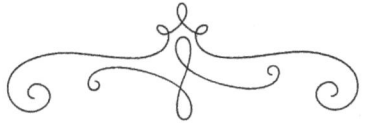

Giovanna

Giovanna

The Cowboy's Calabrese Mail Order Bride

Sweet Land of Liberty Brides
Book 1

Lorena Dove

Printed in the United States of America

First printing, 2017

ISBN-13: 978-0-9964744-1-2
ISBN-09-96474412

Published by Royal Glen Studios, LLC.

www.RoyalGlenStudios.com

Dedication

This book is dedicated in memory of my
great-grandmother,
Giovanna Arlotta D'urso,
who immigrated to the United States
from Reggio di Calabria, Italy, in the
early 20th Century.

.

Acknowledgements

Thank you to my father, who taught me
to love and to never give up.

Preface

Passionate and stubborn, Italian-born Giovanna from Calabria is beautiful, committed to her family, and honest to a fault. Newly widowed, Giovanna must find a way to help her sick daughter, Rosa, before she loses the only one she loves.

Hard-working, reserved and practical, Laars has broken with his Norwegian family to start his own claim in South Dakota. While Laars may think he can do it alone with his cool demeanor and devoted work ethic, in his heart he knows he needs and wants a wife. But is he ready for the sacrifices it takes to lead a ready-made family?

How will Giovanna and Laars be able to forge a life together if they are more devoted to their own needs than to each other?

Giovanna is the first book in the *Sweet Land of Liberty Brides series*, which highlights the courage and travails of first-generation Americans as they brought the customs, language, religion and pride of their native countries to the open lands of the great American west. These hardy and loving people formed the backbone of the young nation as they blended lives together in America's "melting pot."

Thank you for letting me know through your emails, Facebook comments and reviews that my "little stories" bring you joy, laughter, tears and a word of encouragement! It's an honor to have such wonderful readers.

Enjoy your trip back to a simpler time,

LORENA DOVE

~Author of inspirational western romance fiction

Chapter One

"What is your name, child?" asked the large, imposing woman towering over the small creature crouching at the edge of the street. "Goodness gracious, a person could break her ankle stumbling over you!" Mrs. Forsythe waved her handkerchief at her face and peered over her thick glasses.

The small girl froze in place, her hand stretched out toward a dirty biscuit she was trying to scoop up off the sooty, mud-covered street.

"R-R-Rosa," she stammered, looking up with tears in her large brown eyes.

The giant of a woman stood over Rosa, her thin lips set in a grim line, the flowers on her elaborate hat twitching disapproval in time to her shaking head. Rosa cowered beneath her, drawing herself into an even smaller bundle of calico and long black hair. The woman's shadow grew over Rosa as she leaned down. Rosa trembled and closed her eyes tightly shut.

"Rosa. Well then. Ahem," said the woman. "Let me help you with those. Where's your mother?"

Rosa opened her eyes to see the thin lips curled into a genuine smile as Mrs. Forsythe reached across her to retrieve one of the errant biscuits. She burst into tears of relief and self-reproach.

"M-m-mama's inside the church, and I've dropped her basket!"

"Did she buy you all these biscuits?" asked Mrs. Forsythe with one eyebrow raised.

"No, Ma'am! Mama sells biscuits and today I'm helping. Or I'm supposed to be ..." her words trailed off as she fumbled with the ruined goods. "She works hard to bake enough and now these are ruined," Rosa paused to wipe off her tears. "She'll be sad."

Mrs. Susan Forsythe was hardly accustomed to scrambling around in the dirt at the edge of the street. Her normal Sunday practice was to go directly home after church to rest up from her busy week at the milliner's shop, paying no attention to the street vendors who didn't have the money for a permanent stand in the market, much less a spacious storefront like hers.

Whatsoever ye do for the least of these, ye do for Me. The pastor's sermon text echoed in her mind as she considered the dark-haired waif.

"Hand me the basket while you pick up the rest of them," she directed.

"Rosa? Rosa! Where are you?" The rising voice came to their ears across the church courtyard as a petite woman dressed in black rushed about looking this way and that for her daughter.

"Over here!" Mrs. Forsythe waved and pointed down at Rosa.

"What's happened?" Giovanna said in her heavy Italian accent. "Are you hurt, Rosa? The biscuits are covered in soot! *Che sfortuna!* What bad luck!" Giovanna's natural temper and talkativeness were winding up into a tirade.

"I'm sorry, Mama. I stood by the steps liked you asked, but I saw a kitty and thought if I could catch it and bring it home, Pearl would have a friend. I didn't mean to trip and drop the basket, Mama! I'm so very sorry." The tip of Rosa's nose was the only part of her face not streaked with soot or tears as she stood twisting her small hands in her dress.

Giovanna's heart went out to her daughter, so delicate and frail but always concerned about her kitten and any other animal she saw.

"Don't you worry now, Rosa, I can bake some more, and these we can feed to Pearl." Giovanna wiped away Rosa's tears with the apron of her skirt and kissed her tenderly on her forehead.

Rosa buried her face in her mother's black shirtfront, then smiled and looked up at the woman who had helped her.

"Hello! I'm Susan Forsythe," the woman said briskly with her hand outstretched. "When I wasn't tripping over her, I was just helping your daughter with the fallen biscuits."

"Giovanna Ransoni." Taking Mrs. Forsythe's hand, Giovanna tried to make light of her losses even though she hadn't the money for more flour with a day's wages lost in the dirt. "I made these biscuits to sell, but I'm afraid they'll have to be eaten by the animals now."

"Could I buy half your basket right now, if you're selling?"

"God bless you, Ma'am!" Giovanna said, astonished at the generous offer coming from this stern, stout woman. "But they're all broken and dirty."

"Never you mind! I can brush them off and use them for a pudding. Mr. Forsythe will never know," she said with a wink. "On second thought, give me all you have."

Mrs. Forsythe pressed some money into Giovanna's hand and scooped up the biscuits into her shawl, tying them into a tidy pouch. "I don't like to see food go to waste and these look delicious—at least, they did!" With a quick turn to step into her waiting carriage, she called out, "Take care, little Rosa! Good-bye, Giovanna!"

The driver loosened the brake and chucked the reins on the horse's back. As the carriage lurched away from the curb and down the street, Giovanna said, "Rosa, what do the letters say?" She pointed to the sign on the door of the retreating buggy.

"F-O-R—For—S-Y—Forsythe MILL-IN-ER-Y. Forsythe Millinery, Mama." Rosa looked up at her mama and smiled after she puzzled it out.

"*Brava!* Such a smart girl, my Rosa. One day, you'll teach me to read in English, too," Giovanna said. She looked down at the crumple of bills in her hand, pushed them into the pocket under her apron, and hurried home to count them in private.

Chapter Two

*G*iovanna made her way the next morning through the crowded streets of Clarksburg to the other side of town, selling biscuits and looking for the hat maker's shop. She walked down Main St. and crossed the bridge over Elk Creek, enjoying the view of the water rushing by with the West Virginia mountains in the background. So like Calabria, only much greener.

She found a building with a wooden sign hung perpendicular to the street and painted with a jaunty hat. She made out the capital letters F and M. They matched what she had seen on the carriage. She opened the door slowly, intending to just peek inside, only to be announced by a loud ring of a bell.

Mrs. Forsythe's head shot up from her work at the counter.

"May I help you?"

"Good morning, Mrs. Forsythe."

"Oh! Giovanna! Good morning. How is Rosa today?"

"*Bene*, I mean, good, thank you! I brought you freshly baked biscuits since you have paid for them already."

"Why, thank you!" Mrs. Forsythe beamed. "Please, come here and sit."

Not realizing the full extent of the

sacrifice it represented, Mrs. Forsythe was never-the-less intrigued by Giovanna's honesty and work ethic that seemed equal to her own. "Tell me about yourself; I'm rather fascinated to see a mother alone selling biscuits on the streets of Clarksburg. What does your husband do? He must be a lucky man indeed."

"Oh—*mi sposa*," Giovanna swallowed to clear the lump in her throat. "Francesco—Frank—I lost him to the coughing sickness. What do you call it? The doctor said consumption. Rosa was just a baby, and I sell my biscuits now to take care of her." Giovanna looked down at her shoes pointing out from under the dirty hem of her dark dress and sighed. She thought about saying more, but decided against it. "That's all about me," she said quietly.

"Oh! I am sorry," said Mrs. Forsythe. "Well. Surely you have family here then to help you? "

"My husband's brother is helping us; he gave us a room above his store. He is working to bring the rest of the family from Italy. He and Frank came first to America to find work in the mines. Frank and I had just married and he didn't want to come without me. My mama begged me to stay with her until he was settled..." Giovanna's voice trailed off. "Now, I am here with my Rosa." Giovanna again considered saying more about her brother-in-law insisting she pay rent and more for utilities each month, but again kept quiet.

She picked up her basket and stood to go. "You're very kind. Thank you for helping Rosa yesterday and—and for the money," she said, her warm smile returning to her face. "I just wanted to thank you, and now I should be going."

Mrs. Forsythe watched Giovanna make her way out the door and down the street. She was charmed by Giovanna's sad eyes and beautiful smile. Her heart ached for the lonely young woman so far from home, working hard to raise her daughter, and yet grateful and honest.

Chapter Three

Unable to get Giovanna and Rosa off her mind, Mrs. Forsythe took it upon herself to visit them. Giovanna and Rosa lived in a cramped but clean room above her brother-in-law's store in a neighborhood where many had come from Calabria and other regions in the south of Italy.

Giovanna was a busy young woman who used her many skills to eke out a living. She cooked, cleaned, sewed, baked and did chores all while raising a well-mannered daughter without complaint.

She did her best to be a good hostess, making Mrs. Forsythe some tea and offering her a slice of lemon cake out of several she was planning to sell that day. Rosa played quietly nearby with a cloth doll and Pearl curled up on her lap.

"This is delicious, thank you!" Mrs. Forsythe said. "You must be wondering why I've come. I'm worried about Rosa."

Mrs. Forsythe could see that Rosa was a weak child with a cough that racked her thin body, but Giovanna was unable to find the money for anything besides food and the rent her brother-in-law insisted she pay.

Rosa needed to see a doctor, as Giovanna feared her illness would only make her weaker unless diagnosed and treated. Some even said that Rosa was infectious and should be kept locked inside the house, away from other children. This made Giovanna's black eyes flash with anger, but she kept Rosa away from other children to spare her strength.

"I worry, too," Giovanna said. "She's all I have in the world since Frank has gone. We had such plans for our family—a house of our own to raise Rosa in, send her to school, keep her happy .... Now, I just wish for her health and money for the rent," she said quietly.

"You deserve all that and more," Mrs. Forsythe said. "Don't you wish for a man who would take care of you and love you?"

A shy smile crept over Giovanna's face as she looked at the reflection of her twenty-nine-year-old face in the adjacent glass door.

"I do wish for a husband," she said. "But only if that means Rosa will be happier too."

"Of course she would be!" exclaimed Mrs. Forsythe. "Find yourself a man of means who will take care of both of you."

"Who would want to marry a dull-looking widow like me, when Clarksburg is full of beautiful young girls ready for marriage?" cried Giovanna in dismay.

"Then you must go where there aren't so many eligible women. Besides, you're not so dull looking as you believe, if you could get some decent rest." Mrs. Forsythe shuffled some papers up out of the large bag she carried.

"Every week letters arrive at St. Rupert's Church from preachers out West containing excerpts from the matrimonial newspaper in San Francisco." she said. "My own sister answered one, and moved to Kansas City to be married last year." She paused in her excitement, scanning Giovanna's eyes for any sign of interest. Unsatisfied but not dissuaded by her blank expression, Mrs. Forsythe plowed ahead.

"Here look, I've brought you some letters. The light is poor where you're sitting, so I'll read them to you."

Giovanna nodded slightly, and lowered her eyebrows as she strained to listen, grateful that Mrs. Forsythe so tactfully skirted the fact that she couldn't yet read English.

First Mrs. Forsythe read a letter from her sister telling how happy she was as the wife of a man who owned the largest livery in town.

"Now, Giovanna, we're going to read through some of the rest of these and see if there is anyone acceptable," Mrs. Forsythe said. Most were unsuitable to either Giovanna or Mrs. Forsythe, until they came to one that read:

> *No. 258 – A gentleman of 32 years, 5 feet 10 inches, owns a farm outside of town. Desires the companionship of a loving, intelligent and responsible woman between 20 and 28, to take care of his farm and home. Kindly write to Laars Gundersen, c/o Pavente General Store, Faring, Dakota Territory.*

"But it's only for women younger than 28," said Giovanna looking at Mrs. Forsythe in consternation.

"Oh, he'll never be able to tell, Giovanna! How would he know if you're a year or two past his age of preference?" replied Mrs. Forsythe, smiling at Giovanna's honesty. "Now, I think we should start with this one. I'll write whatever you want me to say in reply."

Chapter Four

Giovanna rose at dawn in time to bake fresh biscuits and sell them to the men heading to work. She looked at Rosa sleeping in the bed they shared, and thought about her and Frank's dream of a home of their own as they had travelled to America. Their trip had been delayed until they could save money for two fares, and the ocean journey had been miserable for her at seven months pregnant. Rosa was born early just a few days after they arrived in New York. Then came the journey to Clarksburg and the terrifying sight of Frank becoming weaker with coughing by day and fever each night. By Rosa's first birthday, Giovanna was taking her to visit Frank's grave. Giovanna sighed as she packed her basket, kissed Rosa on the cheek and slipped quietly out the door.

Giovanna returned home at noon and gasped at the sight of her daughter lying sprawled on the floor. She rushed to check her breathing and felt her forehead burning with fever. Sweeping Rosa up in her arms, she ran out of the apartment and down the street to Mr. Vincenza, the druggist. He had given Rosa some medicine once before, but he was no doctor and Giovanna feared it would be too late.

"What now? I'm coming, I'm coming," Mr. Vincenza said to the sound of desperate knocking at the back door of his shop. "Giovanna! What's this?"

Mr. Vincenza swung open the door, took Rosa from her arms and placed her on a small settee. He listened to her breathing and put a cloth with ointment on her chest. Rosa stirred and coughed, but seemed to breathe easier even if she didn't open her eyes.

"Rosa is a very sick child," Mr. Vincenza said. "You can rub this ointment on her chest to help her breathe, but I have nothing for the fever. She should see a doctor. In fact, you should take her to a hospital," he said.

"Rosa, speak to me!" Giovanna cried over her small child. Mr. Vincenza left to greet a customer and Giovanna sat holding Rosa's hand. Rosa's eyes fluttered open for a moment and she smiled at Giovanna, before launching into a new round of coughing that shook her small body.

"I'm going to find a way to take care of you, I promise!" Giovanna whispered through her tears. "Please stay with me, *mi carina*. I'll find a way."

.

Chapter Five

Laars Gundersen drove back to his farm with gold in his shirt pocket. Not real gold, but the solid feeling just the same of a stronger future. He'd finally received a letter from a woman who could become his wife. He'd glanced over it quickly in town, and now as he entered his sparsely furnished home, he hurried to his reading chair to take his time and study it.

Giovanna. He said the strange name a few times in his mind, then spoke it out loud. "Giovanna." So different sounding from the Ilsas and Ingrids he knew in the close-knit Norwegian community he came from in Minnesota.

Dear Mr. Gundersen, the letter began. He leaned back and pictured her writing at a small table under a dim lamp, holding the pen and thinking hard just as he had when he wrote the ad. He read that she was widowed and caring for her four-year-old daughter, Rosa. She boasted about her skills, her ability to work hard, and her love of her new country. Any man would be happy to see such a response and Laars was overwhelmed at his good fortune. He reached for his writing box and took up his pen.

Dear Giovanna,

I was fascinated to hear about you, an industrious woman indeed. I am impressed by your skills and energy. With all confidence that as much as I know is fair, I would like you to come meet me, see my claim and be my wife. It's not an easy life but a good one here in the Dakota territory. Together we'll work my claim and I'll look after you. I hope to find in you as suitable a companion as you will in me.

Please use this money to arrange travel for yourself and Rosa to Kansas City and on to Sioux Falls. From there, the stationmaster will put you on a coach to Faring. Let me know your date of arrival and I will come to town to retrieve you.

Yours only,

Laars Gundersen

Laars read over his offer. He was a man of few words but wanted to make sure he said everything. He had never considered having a child in the house so soon, and wondered about bringing a woman of such a different background to Faring. Here, almost everyone he knew had come from Norway or been born in Minnesota soon after their parents had arrived. His family and relatives worked hard, happy to have land of their own to farm since it was difficult if not impossible to find in Norway.

He crossed the barewood floor of his kitchen and set his coffee cup in the metal pan that served as a sink. He thought about the girls back in Minnesota he knew, of how reluctant they were to move further west. They all seemed happy staying within a few miles of their parents.

But Laars had wanted more. A

chance to build a bigger farm—and a place to tame for his own.

He knew the Pavente's who owned the store were from Italy. They were friendly even if they sometimes made his head hurt by talking all at once. He saw how hard they worked and loved their families. He could picture himself with beautiful, dark-haired Giovanna at his side.

He couldn't know that Giovanna had dictated the letter to Mrs. Forsythe, who edited her words as she wrote, taking out her fear and anguish over Rosa's health. She wrote a letter true to reality but devoid of the turmoil of emotions that filled Giovanna's heart.

Chapter Six

Giovanna was overawed. Mrs. Forsythe had read her the letter from Laars, and sent back her acceptance. She looked up to the sky with thanks, thankful for God's benevolence. All night she thought about her life as the wife of a cattleman. She thought of Rosa, getting better and growing up on a farm in Dakota. She could send Rosa to a nice school and she would be at home to take care of her.

Maybe, if it wasn't too much to ask, she wouldn't be lonely anymore. She wished for love and for a man who would love Rosa as much as she did. She hoped that man was Laars Gundersen.

Giovanna wound up her business in Clarksburg within days. She tearfully visited Frank's grave for the last time. She bid an emotional farewell to Mrs. Forsythe, and a quieter one to Frank's brother, promising them she would write. Finally with her few possessions packed in a trunk, she sat on a bench at the railway station with Rosa, thinking of her life.

For the second time she was leaving a home she knew to venture further away from anything she knew or loved. The mountains of West Virginia had comforted her in her grief after losing Frank, and given her strength when she didn't think she could go on caring for Rosa alone.

She boarded the train feeling nauseous and fighting back an overwhelming fear. The jolt of the train as it pulled out of the station released a flood of tears. Her heart was torn by the strange new hope for Rosa, a feeling of freedom, and sadness mixed with love for the home she had made since Frank's death. She might never come back to Clarksburg again.

As the train pulled into Sioux Falls, Giovanna and Rosa boarded the stage to Faring. Giovanna settled in and introduced herself to the young woman sharing the coach.

"Nice to meet you," the woman replied. "I'm Jane Snyder. I've never seen you around town before."

"I am just now moving here," replied Giovanna, not sure of how to explain her circumstances to a complete stranger.

"Please don't mind my abruptness, but are you here to contract marriage?" Jane put the question as politely as she could.

"Yes-s," Giovanna stammered. She didn't realize it would be so obvious. "I've been corresponding with a man who staked a claim."

Jane shifted a bit in her seat. "I must warn you. You seem to be a sweet girl, but the men here in Dakota attract all sorts of women from the East with a promise to marry them. Why, I've heard of cases where the women were told outright lies! They could have promised to marry a downright mean man, or even an actual bandit!" Jane's eyes flashed at the thought. "Well, I hope yours isn't like that," she finished.

"Thank you for your concern," Giovanna said and turned to look out the window, heart pumping and her stomach twisting in knots. She thought of Clarksburg and her life that she knew, hard as it had been. Maybe it had been foolish to leave and take this risk with Rosa. She stroked Rosa's hair as she slept in her lap. *My sweet child.* Rosa had learned to not bother her mother with many questions and she trusted Giovanna completely. She was frail yet mature for her age, as she sought not to add to the stresses her mother faced.

As the miles wore on, Giovanna imagined the worst for herself. She feared the shame and dishonor that would come to her if Laars had been lying. She was worried for Rosa and her safety. By the time the driver opened the door and she climbed out of the stage, she had to force back tears and take control of her sinking heart as her eyes searched for Laars.

A tall figure emerged from the sparse crowd coming towards her. Tall, blonde and a little shabby-looking, Laars came forward smiling to greet her.

"Welcome!" he said, his broad, open face covered in a big grin. "The Dakota Territory has awaited you, Giovanna."

Giovanna returned a faint smile through an exhausted haze. She gave him her hand as the other instinctively hugged Rosa to her side.

Laars politely shook Giovanna's hand, not taking any notice of Rosa. "You must be so tired from your trip! It's only a few miles more to the claim. Let me get your luggage. "

Laars pointed out the roads and landmarks as he drove them in his horse and cart out to the claim. Giovanna stared bleakly at the stark landscape with a sky so huge she felt more lost than ever. He pulled up to a small square home with two outbuildings. Laars had enlarged it from the initial shack he had built on the claim two years ago. It now had a kitchen with a wood stove and room for a table, a sitting room with another small stove, two rooms for sleeping, and a small porch.

"Well, here's Rosa's room, and yours until—well, you know," he said nervously. "Until we are married. My father is coming to stay with us tonight."

"Thank you," Giovanna said weakly. "Do you mind if we wash up?"

"Of course! Please rest a while. I have some chores to do before my family arrives to meet you." Laars closed the door and Giovanna heard his heavy footsteps walk away toward the kitchen.

Giovanna washed her face and hands in the basin, and dampened a cloth to wipe Rosa's face. They lay together on the bed, and Rosa immediately fell asleep. Giovanna closed her eyes, trying to rest, but all she could do was wipe tears from her eyes as an avalanche of fear flooded her mind.

Chapter Seven

"What do you think of her, son?" Mr. Gundersen asked Laars as they waited for Giovanna to come out of her room for dinner. "I hope you have done the right thing, considering the ladies in Minnesota that might have made a match with you."

"Father, we've been over this before," Laars said. "They are happy in Minnesota. I was happy there, too, as a child. But just as you left home for new lands, I have my own dream of what I want in life."

"Ya, I see," Mr. Gundersen said. "We left our home country to find new land and homes for ourselves, and our families. We didn't leave to have our own family permanently scattered to the winds. You know, son, you may go where you want, but you cannot escape yourself."

"Yes, Father, I know but—"

Laars was grateful for the light footsteps that interrupted the same conversation he had every time he spoke with his father. Giovanna stood quietly in the doorway, little Rosa shyly looking out from behind her skirts.

Laars jumped up and Mr. Gundersen rose stiffly to greet them. "Giovanna, you look—" he paused at the sight of her puffy eyes and red nose. "...a bit tired still. Father, this is Giovanna."

"Very pleased to meet you," Giovanna said as she looked up at Mr. Gundersen. "This is my daughter, Rosa," she said as Rosa hid her face. Giovanna drew herself up to her full height of five feet, three inches. She was like a small cat eyeing two large, but gentle, bears. The men's heads nearly touched the ceiling as they towered over.

"Hallo," Mr. Gundersen said, shook her hand, and returned to his seat.

"Well–uh–would you like some tea? The ladies are waiting in the kitchen to meet you," Laars said.

Some of Laars's family had come for the wedding the next day. His married sister, Ilsa, her family and two cousins were staying at the boarding house in Faring. Even Laars's 11-year-old niece Anna was taller than Giovanna. Their blonde hair, blue eyes and fair skin were a marvel to her. Their white blouses were decorated with intricate embroidery, and they passed plates of salted fish, bread, cheese and *krumkaker*.

"Look, Mama," Rosa whispered, pointing at the thin, rolled up cookies covered in powdered sugar. "Can I try one?"

"Yes, dear. They look much like the *pizzelle* we make at Christmastime," Giovanna whispered back. It will be good to have some baking pans again, Giovanna thought.

They asked her polite questions, speaking in low tones, one at a time, with pauses that seemed like ages between sentences. Not at all like Frank's family, around whom Giovanna could hardly get a word in.

As the night wore on, Mr. Gundersen took up a fiddle, and the family sang songs together. Giovanna couldn't understand the Norwegian folk songs, but she found herself picking up the words when they started a happy American tune:

Ho! Westward!

Soon the world shall know

That all is grand

In the western land;

Ho! Westward Ho!

The family sang, celebrating Laars's and Giovanna's wedding. Though different from her own family, Giovanna's sense of fear retreated in their gentle presence. Rosa looked happy, and the women remarked about her beautiful dark hair and eyes.

Mr. Gundersen kept a careful watch on Giovanna before retiring for the night to Laars's room, and finally the others left, promising to see them at the church the next day.

Laars and Giovanna stood together awkwardly before the door to her room.

"Is there anything I can get for you?" said Laars, searching for a hint of responsiveness in Giovanna's eyes.

She smiled and met his gaze. "Well, I'm just a little tired with all the travel I suppose." She struggled to conceal the doubts from her face, worried that if Laars knew she was crying in fear earlier, he wouldn't go through with the marriage.

"I hope you're happy with the house—and with me. I'm sure you'll feel better by morning. After all, it's our wedding day!" said Laars.

"Yes, of course!" Giovanna replied trying hard to sound convincing this time. "Well, good night. Sleep well!"

Giovanna quickly stepped into her room and closed the door. Undressing quietly so as not to wake Rosa, she slipped in beside her and fell asleep, her dreams full of train whistles, people waving good-bye, Frank's face, singing, and church bells.

Chapter Eight

I n the morning, Giovanna dressed carefully in the new blue gown given to her by Mrs. Forsythe.

"You can't be married in your widow's black," she had huffed when Giovanna protested the gift. She carefully unfolded the white shawl she had worn as a veil her first time as a bride. Given to her by her grandmother in Italy, it was one of the only possessions she had left from her life in Calabria.

Mr. Gundersen, Laars, Giovanna and Rosa drove silently to the church. His family sat in two pews on the right side of the aisle, while Rosa sat with the minister's wife behind Giovanna.

After the minister pronounced them man and wife, Giovanna waited for Laars to take her hand and lead her to the altar, where they would kneel and receive Communion and a blessing, as called for in Giovanna's Roman Catholic tradition.

Instead, Laars, took her hand, and turned around to the sparse gathering as the preacher said: "I now pronounce you man and wife! Well, go ahead and kiss her!"

Giovanna smiled even as she shivered. *I will begin marriage without absolution, God forgive me!* She stood still as Laars reached to lift up her veil.

Her eyes met his, and in their pleading he stopped halfway bent toward her, and planted his mouth politely on her cheek. He stood straight, and smiled ruefully at her obvious relief.

"Congratulations!" Mr. Gundersen came forward and took Giovanna's hands in his. "You will be a strong wife for my Laars. He will need some reigning in ...."

The group walked down the street to the boarding house parlor. Mrs. Svenson had put out a pitcher of lemonade and glasses and arranged small cakes on a porcelain platter.

"I hope you will be happy, Giovanna," said Ilsa. "Laars has always been ... a little different. I'm sure you'll be fine together."

"Yes, thank you," Giovanna said. She couldn't help asking, "Does he like children, do you know?"

"Children? Laars?" Ilsa said with a sniff. "Well, he likes them all right, I suppose. I've never heard him mention them. He hardly looks at my Johan or Anna. But then, he's always had nothing but land and cattle on his mind that I could tell. It drove several of the girls back home quite to distraction."

She moved away and called to her children and husband. "Come now, we should be heading to the station."

Why would he want me if he doesn't like children? Giovanna's eyes scanned the room for Rosa and found her sitting quietly next to Anna, enjoying the older girl's attention. At her mother's call, Anna stood and gave Rosa a quick hug before leaving.

"Mama, I like her," Rosa whispered as she came next to Giovanna. "Can we visit her in Minnesota some day?"

"I hope so, dear. I do hope so," Giovanna said before taking her place next to Laars to bid good-bye to her new relatives.

Chapter Nine

Mr. Gundersen stayed at the claim for a few days helping Laars finish a fence. He stayed in Laars's room while Giovanna and Rosa continued to share the other. Laars slept on a pallet in the sitting room that he took up each day before he went out to do the morning chores.

Giovanna poured Mr. Gundersen a cup of coffee. She was starting to get used to the quiet ways of the Gundersen men. At first it had unnerved her, but the long silences made it easier to keep her emotions in check.

"I'll be leaving tomorrow," Mr. Gundersen said in his matter-of-fact way. She nodded and turned to the stove, surprised a bit when she heard him clear his throat and continue.

"Laars was the hardest of all my children," he said. "He had a mind of his own and was careless, too. His mother and I worried a lot about him. We raised him the same as the others, but he didn't want to stay with the family. I thought it was foolish for him to move to Dakota on his own. I can rest a little easier now knowing he has you to look after him."

Giovanna smiled to herself at the idea that her small presence could ease his father's mind.

"Laars grew so fast. That's how a middle child grows, unnoticed," the old man laughed at his own remark, and she laughed with him.

"What about children?" she asked. "Do you think Laars likes children?"

"I'm afraid he's not too taken with children, my dear. But neither was I at his age, until I had children of my own."

Giovanna's hand stopped in mid-wipe of the stove at the words and she let out a small sigh.

"I know you ask this with your Rosa in mind, and I fear Rosa is a responsibility that Laars was not ready to take yet. I believe he over-estimated himself, as usual." He paused and tried to soften his words. "I'm not sure how it will turn out, but Rosa is a well-mannered child. Hopefully, Laars will be at peace with her."

Giovanna didn't know what to say. What was the old man implying? What did he mean by being "at peace with her?" She nodded, gave him a faded smile and went off to check on Rosa.

She spent the night thinking about it as Laars and Mr. Gundersen talked of the work still to be done on the claim. She was tired of being worried; she wished she could talk to someone who understood. Tomorrow Mr. Gundersen would be gone and she would be alone with Laars. She would have to move into his room, yet he still felt like a complete stranger to her.

What was she doing here? *Rosa.* Rosa was all she worried about now. *Will Laars ever be able to love Rosa?* She didn't stop to wonder whether he would ever love her.

With Mr. Gundersen gone, there would be time to get to know Laars better and find out for herself whether he could love Rosa. She wanted to appear strong and happy, the way Mrs. Forsythe had represented her positivity and energy in her letters. She fell asleep determined not to disappoint Laars with her worries, but to first prove herself as a valuable partner before seeking help for Rosa.

Chapter Ten

The next morning, Laars drove Mr. Gundersen to the stage leaving Giovanna and Rosa at home. The claim was theirs now. In three more years, Laars and Giovanna would own it outright. She was married and in charge of taking care of him and the house. This she knew how to do. She got busy straightening up the small kitchen before sitting down to braid Rosa's hair.

"Ouch, Mama! That hurts," Rosa said as Giovanna pulled the separated lengths of her hair tightly into the braid.

"Sorry, child, I need your hair to stay like this all day; I don't have time to brush out the tangles later," she said.

"I'm sorry. I know you're busy," Rosa said sweetly and kissed her mother on the cheek.

Giovanna watched Rosa gingerly make her way across the yard to play near the shed. She had so much to do to make the small house feel more home-like. Laars had promised her some material for curtains in the window after she convinced him it would keep the place cooler in summer and warmer in winter.

She worried that with the travel, the wedding and taking care of the Gundersen men she hadn't spent as much time with Rosa as she should. The child spent her days reading a couple of small books Mrs. Forsythe had given her. She missed Pearl, and Giovanna had promised her a new kitten, though she wondered whether Laars would allow it. She would make sure to keep Rosa happy. Rosa was the reason she had left the beautiful mountains, wasn't she?

She remembered Mrs. Forsythe's words: she should find a man to love her and take care of her. Was she really here for Rosa or was she here to find love and overcome her loneliness for Frank? She wasn't sure. Rosa was all she had. Her love for her daughter was the most priceless, precious and irreplaceable feeling. How could anyone, especially Laars, replace Frank and Rosa in her heart?

Rosa will be happier here, and if she is happy, I'll be happy. She'd never let anything change that.

Laars was anxious to acquaint Giovanna with all the work to do on the claim. He needed her help in more ways than just making curtains and meals, as much as he appreciated them.

He carefully showed her how to put hay out for the cattle once winter came, and explained how they would need to check all of their cattle several times a week throughout the year. He would slowly build up the herd by selling the best ones each year and until he could buy his own bull steer. Right now, he had to take his cows two at a time to a ranch 20 miles away for breeding.

"By spring, the cows will be ready to calve, so we'll have to check them daily," he said.

He told her that in the spring and summer they would cull the herd and cut hay. The majority of his calves sold through auction and left mid-August. A few were sold throughout the year.

"Giovanna ... Giovanna?" He thought she had been listening carefully but saw that she hadn't heard the last of his words. He worried the chores were boring to her. She had spent her life in the city, socializing, baking and moving around among crowds. Maybe open fields and silent animals weren't as exciting, but it was their future.

Startled by his stern look, Giovanna spoke up. "Yes, the calves," she struggled to remember the last thing she had heard him say. "I hope I'll be as much of a help to you as you expect."

Laars scanned her face for the truth and his eyes softened. She was so mysterious, with her faraway look that only left her face when he spoke directly to her. His eyes roamed over her, taking in her full red lips and violet eyes behind dark lashes. Her soft neck exposed as she looked up at him made him want to plaster it with warm kisses. He felt a stirring in his heart and reached out to her.

He brought her hand to his lips and kissed it gently. "Jo. May I call you Jo?"

The husky sound of his voice took her by surprise. She had never seen his bright blue eyes look so full. They normally darted about flashing with thoughts of all the work to be done.

"Y-yes," was all she could manage to reply.

He drew her toward him and reached down to place a gentle kiss on her lips, breaking away silently to look at her again.

She felt a blush of warmth rise inside her, her chest and cheeks flushing. Was Laars falling in love with her? Was the shine in his eyes real? Her heart beat uncomfortably in her chest as she struggled to reconcile this long-ago feeling with a new man.

An image of Frank flashed before her, and Giovanna pulled away her hand and stepped back, trying to return to an equilibrium that now seemed impossible to find.

Embarrassed by her retreat, Laars looked away and fumbled a bit with a stall door before heading inside to check on one of his cows. Her shocked eyes made him feel he had done something wrong. He knew he could make her love him, but it would take time. He couldn't tell what she wanted from him; she never let him get too close, yet she seemed to fear losing him. He didn't know if he could ever understand Giovanna.

Chapter Eleven

iovanna's cheeks were still warm as she made her way through the rough grass back to the house. It was the first time she and Laars had been alone, and when she understood the beginning of desire in his eyes, the reminiscence of love and longing it brought so quickly to her heart had overwhelmed her mind and senses.

Could she feel love for Laars, so soon after meeting him? With Mr.

Gundersen gone, she would be sleeping for the first time in his room tonight. Surely he won't expect me to love him so soon.

Closing the door to the kitchen, Giovanna quickly went to work adding dry sticks of wood to the stove to bring the temperature up under the stew pot. She peeked under the tea towel covering her rising bread loaf, and then turned it into the one tin pan to bake it in the small oven compartment.

Rosa lay curled up asleep in Laars's reading chair with her book on her chest. Giovanna quietly checked on her, concerned for the rattling breaths she was taking. Not wanting to disturb her rest, Giovanna said a quick prayer over Rosa before turning back to set out three plates at the table.

A few heavy footsteps crossed the floor as Laars made his way in from the shed. He went to the basin, poured water in from the pitcher, splashed water on his face and rubbed his hands together.

"Laars, I—dinner will be ready soon," Giovanna stammered.

"I see that," he said quietly before turning around.

Something about the way his muscles moved on his forearms as he haphazardly dried his hands with the bread towel brought the fluttering feeling back to Giovanna's heart. Subconsciously tapping her hand to her chest, she moved to open the oven door.

"Here, you'll need this," Laars said, handing her the towel. He watched her skillfully pull the bread from the hot oven and quickly turn it out onto the wooden sideboard. The warm, yeasty smell rose to his nose and he took in a big breath.

"Ahh, it's been a long time since I had a hot loaf to eat with my supper. It looks wonderful and smells even better! You're a good cook, Jo."

At the sound of his name for her, she looked at him and smiled. This, too, would take getting used to, but Giovanna felt a flush of pride in her chest.

Laars stopped in the sitting room and stared at Rosa sleeping in his chair. He turned to say something to Giovanna, thought better of it, and continued to his room.

Giovanna went to gently shake Rosa awake. Her arm was too warm, and Giovanna quickly felt her forehead and put an ear to her chest.

"Rosa, Rosa, can you wake for supper?"

"Oohh, Mama," Rosa's black eyes flickered open and her body spasmed in short, throaty coughs. "I was dreaming that Pearl was looking for me. Do you think Mrs. Forsythe is cuddling her the way she likes?"

"Pearl is almost a full-grown cat now, my dear," Giovanna said. "I'm sure she's happy keeping the mice away from the flowers and feathers in Mrs. Forsythe's hats."

Rosa giggled at the thought, straightened herself and came to the table. "You've already set out the plates, Mama. That's my job! I'll get the forks and napkins."

Laars noticed the smile on Giovanna's face when he returned in a clean shirt. *She looks so young and free when she smiles.*

The young family ate dinner in near silence, punctuated only by the sound of Rosa coughing between small bites of food. Laars's eyes flashed the first time, and by the fourth or fifth time he raised a questioning eyebrow to Giovanna.

She shook her head worriedly and shrugged her shoulders, trying to make light of Rosa's poor health.

"She's just worn out from our travels. I'll put her straight to bed and clean up later."

Giovanna bundled her daughter off to their room, puzzled by Laars's lack of concern other than obviously for himself that Rosa wasn't well. Giovanna slipped Rosa's dress over her head and tucked her under the covers wearing her soft cotton shift. Rosa's eyes were glazed as she smiled at her mother before closing them to sleep.

As Giovanna closed the door, she saw Laars's shadow in his room. She paused before returning to clean the dishes with hot water poured from a kettle on the warm stove. *In a little while, he'll be asleep. Then I can change in Rosa's room before—* Her mind came up with a blank. Before what? She hadn't allowed herself to consider the moment when she would have to join her new husband in his bed.

Laars listened to Giovanna's movements about the kitchen. He was a man, but it wasn't his way to press a woman for affection. By the look on her face when he had kissed her earlier, he knew it would take time. Finally, she appeared at the doorway.

"It's all right, Jo," Laars said. "There's plenty of room for you. I'll stay to my side and you'll sleep peacefully."

Giovanna let out her breath and quietly came into the room. Turning her back in the darkness, she undid the buttons of her dress, quickly slid it down, adjusted the shoulders of her shift and slipped under the blanket at the very edge of the bed. She made herself as small as she could.

Laars stared up at the ceiling. "Good night, dear Jo," he said.

"Good night—" Giovanna's voice was drowned out by the sound of coughing coming from Rosa's room.

"How long has she been sick?" Laars asked. "Is she contagious?"

"No! Else I would be sick by now, too," Giovanna answered. "She's just tired from her travels." Giovanna was glad Laars was finally asking about Rosa's health, even if he seemed indifferent.

Laars rolled over, but as the coughing continued, his voice took on a sharper tone. "There's a lot to be done tomorrow and I need my sleep, Giovanna. Is there something you can give her?"

Giovanna sat up on the side of the bed. "I'll go to her. She hasn't slept alone in her whole life. Maybe I can keep her quiet."

Giovanna left the room in relief and quietly went to Rosa.

Chapter Twelve

By morning, Rosa's fever was worse. Giovanna came to the kitchen to start breakfast. Laars was already at the shed. *I must tell him over breakfast that I need to get help for Rosa.*

She made coffee and put a pan of biscuits in the oven. Best to talk to a man with a full stomach, her grandmother always said. *Il pane apre tutte le bocche.* Bread opens all mouths.

When Laars came in, she had biscuits and gravy on the table, and poured him a cup of coffee. With a short nod of his head, he folded his hands and said a silent prayer.

"Sit, eat," he said with his mouth full, pointing with his knife at the chair.

Rosa took a breath and sat down across from Laars. She brought the coffee cup to her lips and took a half sip to warm her throat.

"Laars, I know it's sudden, but I'm worried about Rosa. I need to take her to town to a druggist today and get some salve for her chest."

Laars looked up sharply and studied her face. "A druggist? Faring isn't Clarksburg. We have whatever the Pavantes have at the general store."

"Well in any case, they'll have what I need for her. Except what she really needs is—" Giovanna's voice cracked.

"Go on." Laars's blue eyes were looking right through her.

Startled by his icy expression, Giovanna struggled to continue. "What she really needs is to see a doctor." There. She had said it.

"A doctor! And how much is the doctor then, Giovanna?" Laars was starting to become agitated. "How long have you known Rosa needed to see a doctor?"

Giovanna's face fell as she heard him call her by her full name. At the same time, anger rose in her as he so callously discussed her daughter's very life.

"I told you—in my letter! The druggist in Clarksburg said she needed to see a doctor a month ago. I assume you have been planning for it since we arrived."

"A month ago. That would be—let's see—right before you sent me your first letter. A letter that said nothing about Rosa being sick."

"What?" Giovanna faced him, her dark eyes flashing. "Of course I wrote about it, well at least, I said it—" Giovanna stopped in mid-sentence as she remembered Mrs. Forsythe writing the letter for her. What else did she leave out?

"Her condition is not serious if she could just get the right medicine. I had to have some reason to leave my home and what was left of my family in Clarksburg, didn't I?" She fought to control her tongue, but the pressure of worry and the muted emotions she had kept to fit in to the Gundersen family finally broke free.

"I see. All right, then." Laars pushed his chair back from the table and stood. He towered over her and his silence felt like a cloud above her. He started to speak, then turned to head for the door. "I'll get the wagon."

Laars didn't say another word the entire 8 miles into town. Giovanna sat with Rosa wrapped in a blanket on her lap, even though the heat of her skin and weight of her in the blanket was making Giovanna sweat. Rosa's skin was dry and she had only opened her eyes once when Giovanna put her dress on over her head.

"Shh, shhh, *mi carina.* Everything will be all right," Giovanna whispered to her between her prayers. Whatever would come of Laars's anger with her over not telling him about Rosa's condition, she would handle later. Once Rosa was well, Laars would come to know how lovely and sweet she was, and he would come to love her. Giovanna could only hope and pray.

Chapter Thirteen

"My goodness, I was wondering when this lunk would bring you by to see me!" The sweet sound of Mrs. Pavente's heavily accented voice came to Giovanna's ears as soon as they stepped in to the store. "Laars Gundersen, what a beautiful young wife you have!"

"'Mornin', Mrs. Pavente," Laars said, ignoring her pleasantries. "Giovanna here—Mrs. Gundersen—will be needing some medicinal salve for the child."

Laars's stiff introduction would never do for Mrs. Pavente.

"Oh my dear, come right here, bring her to me," she said and rushed to Giovanna's side to help her carry Rosa. Feeling the heat of the limp girl in the blanket, Mrs. Pavente looked into Giovanna's worried face.

"*Dio mio*, she's burning up with fever. Follow me."

Giovanna followed Mrs. Pavente to the back of the store and up a small flight of steps. Mrs. Pavente opened the door to a sparsely furnished room at the top of the stairs, with a table, lantern and small cot. Giovanna laid Rosa on the coverlet and slowly unwrapped the blanket from around her.

"She's been coughing all night, and this morning her fever hasn't come down," Giovanna said. "Please, can you help her?"

Mrs. Pavente was already pouring water into a basin and wringing out a small cloth to place on Rosa's forehead.

"There, there. I have some salve in the store we'll put on her chest, poor thing. And it's fortunate, too, that Dr. Ledville is coming today to pick up a delivery."

"Oh, thank goodness," Giovanna said. "Only, I don't have money for a doctor."

"No money! And you, married to Laars Gundersen! I happen to know, he has money enough for an emergency like this. Now you go down and look next to the candy counter for the shelf with blue bottles and ointments. Bring me the small jar on the end."

Giovanna descended the steps to the store and crossed over next to the candy counter. Laars came to her side.

"Well?" he asked.

"Mrs. Pavente is trying to cool her down and if we could, we need to buy this salve." Giovanna scanned the wooden shelf and found the jar Mrs. Pavente needed. "That is, if it is ok with you."

"It'll have to be ok, it's what we came for, isn't it?" Laars said. "Look, Giovanna, yes, I can pay for it and I've spoken to Mr. Pavente to add your name on my store account so you can get the things you need when we are in town. I have some money saved, but it's for the hay and grain we need for the animals this winter, and a new hub and wheel for the wagon, and an addition on the shed, and a new gate for the fence..." He stopped when he saw the alarmed look on her face.

"Oh, Laars! How can I thank you? But please, I beg you, Mrs. Pavente says the doctor will be here today! Can I please stay with Rosa so he can see her?" Giovanna had never begged for anything in her life, and never would, for herself.

Laars's broad shoulders bent down towards her and he drew her against his chest. Giovanna had been strong for a long time, on her own. She had lied to him by not telling him about Rosa's illness. He hadn't even wanted a wife who already had a child. And yet ... the pleading look in her eyes: it shouldn't be there. He liked the spark he saw as she defended her actions earlier better than this. If she was hurting, he would take care of her. And if she needed his help for Rosa, he would give her whatever he could.

The realization of his love for her gripped his throat. "Jo," was all he could say as he stroked her hair.

Chapter Fourteen

"It's settled then, Pavente. Tell the doctor I'm good for the money," Laars said as he readied to head back to the claim. "I'll be back tomorrow for Giovanna and Rosa, and thank you for letting them stay tonight," he said.

Giovanna paced the upstairs room where Rosa lay, looking every few minutes out the window for Dr. Ledville. Finally, a single horse pulling a beautiful black carriage came into view, driven by a man with a black coat, tall black hat, and large leather bag on the seat next to him. She ran down the steps in time to hear Mrs. Pavente's greeting.

"Dr. Ledville, we are in need of you today! We have your order, right here ready to go for you. But if you please—"

"Dr. Ledville? I'm Giovanna Gundersen," she said, rushing headlong up to the astonished gentleman. "Please, sir, will you come upstairs? It's my daughter."

"My, little lady, we are in quite the rush. Hmm, Gundersen, eh?" Dr. Ledville took mental inventory of the patients he had in Faring. "I haven't treated a Gundersen before, have I, Pavente?"

"No, *Dottore*. It's ok; her husband is a good man. I have his word on it for you. He pays his account on time and asked you to please look at the child."

"Well, in that case," Dr. Ledville took off his coat and handed it to Mrs. Pavente. "Lead the way, Mrs. Gundersen."

Dr. Ledville's jocularity left him as soon as he saw Rosa lying on the bed. He listened to her chest, and had her sit up and cough for him.

"Very bad, it's very bad indeed," he told Giovanna gravely. "This child needs treatment beyond what ointments can provide. There's a sanitarium in Sioux Falls and she must be transported there at morning light."

Dr. Ledville stopped. *If she makes it.*

Giovanna's face fell and a cry of grief poured from her. "Oh, my poor Rosa, I'm so sorry," she said. She put her face in her hands and let herself feel the full shock.

Dr. Ledville stood quietly and finally put a hand on her arm.

"Don't worry, my dear. I'll do the best I can for her."

"Doctor, can I accompany her?" Giovanna's voice was so quiet he bent his head to hear her.

"It isn't wise," he said gently. "We can't know what other illness you might be exposed to. It's best if I take her, and you can come to see her in a few days' time."

"What's this?" Mrs. Pavente was at the doorway. Seeing Giovanna's face, she took her in her arms. "There, there. You stay by me a day or so. I can use the help, and it will be easier for you to travel from here."

Dr. Ledville made his way out, leaving the two women alone.

"She's all that I have," Giovanna said, her eyes brimming with tears.

"All? You have a fine husband, and…"

"She's all that is mine! All that's left from my Frank," Giovanna unburdened herself and slumped down on the cot next to Rosa's still form.

"You will never forget your first love; that is true." Mrs. Pavente said. "*Tempo, marito e figli*—Weather husbands and children—we must take them as they come."

Giovanna nodded at the familiar saying. Her own mother had said the same when Giovanna discovered she was pregnant with Rosa before her trip to America.

"Now Laars Gundersen is a fine man. Your heart will learn to love him soon enough. In the meantime, he's treating the child as his own. Although it's going to be a bit of a blow for him to hear that she must be in a hospital. What's needed is needed. You will find a way."

Giovanna gratefully accepted Mrs. Pavente's words and prayed. *Please let Laars agree to the hospital. I'll pay for it myself if I have to.*

Chapter Fifteen

The next morning, Giovanna kept a brave face saying good-bye to Dr. Ledville and kissing and holding Rosa as long as she could. Rosa could say nothing but smiled faintly at her mother.

"I'll be right beside you soon, my darling," Giovanna whispered. "May God go with you." She pulled off her grandmother's white shawl and laid it over Rosa. As the carriage pulled onto the road, Giovanna stood in shock watching it take with it all that she loved in the world.

As the carriage started out down the road, Mrs. Pavente held Giovanna back, fearing the distraught mother would race after it.

She made the sign of the cross as she helped Giovanna back into the store. "Come now, Giovanna," she clucked. "She will get good care now. We must pray for God's help and the angels to protect her."

"She'll be scared without me. I should have gone with her! What am I going to do?"

"When we don't know what to do, we must do the next thing in front of us that needs to be done. Right now, you can help me clean the store. Mr. Pavente is not as careful as I like, and it needs to be straightened." Mrs. Pavente wanted to keep busy herself.

Laars arrived at noon and tied up the horse to the post in front of the store. Ducking his head under the door, he called out to Mr. Pavente.

"Pavente! I'm back to fetch my wife. Tell her—" He stopped short seeing Giovanna wearing an apron with broom in hand.

"Laars, I'm so glad to see you," she said, coming toward him. "Dr. Ledville has taken Rosa with him and I don't know what I'll do if she doesn't get well!"

"Taken her? Where?"

"To his house in Springvale and on to the hospital in Sioux Falls so she can be treated."

"The hospital! Pavente! I didn't approve of this!" Laars's blue eyes had turned a smoky color and redness had crept up from his neck and spread to his cheeks.

"Giovanna, we can't afford this. What were you thinking?"

Giovanna saw her husband's angry face and dropped the broom. Turning away, she ran up the stairs to the little room and shut the door.

"Laars Gundersen, have you no heart?" Mrs. Pavente said. "The poor woman is worried sick about Rosa. Did you even think to ask if she would get well?"

Laars stood staring at the place where Giovanna had been.

"And she is helping me to keep your account low, is that not a good wife?" Mrs. Pavente continued.

"If anyone needs help, it is me, on the claim," Laars said. "Tell her to meet me outside." His eyes had changed to a look of defeat. He turned on his heel and left the store.

Mrs. Pavente started to speak, but at her husband's look, she closed her mouth.

Mr. Pavente took off his apron and went outside. Laars was roughly checking the laces on his horse and about to step up into the wagon.

"I see the new buckles are holding up well," Mr. Pavente said.

"Mm-hmm," Laars allowed.

"Those are the best ones I carry," Mr. Pavente said.

Laars looked up from the horse. "Yes, that's what you told me when I bought them. You were right."

Mr. Pavente took out his handkerchief and polished his glasses. When he was finished, he put them back on and wiped his forehead. As he carefully folded the cloth before returning it to his pocket, he said, "Laars, I tell you straight, about everything, right? You've been married what, all of a week now?"

Laars considered. "Almost."

"Good, good. Me? I've been married going on 30 years. Mrs. Pavente, she's a real woman. Left her mama and her sisters and moved across this great country with me. She works in the store and takes care of me. We had five children before we were married eight years. Two of them are gone now. And mostly, she never complains. We laugh, we cry, we have everything we need. We didn't love each other at first, but we learned to."

Again the redness began to creep up Laars's face from the neck up. He wasn't used to hearing such personal details from the shopkeeper.

Mr. Pavente took no notice. "Take it from me. Your Giovanna, she's-a strong like this." Mr. Pavente held his hand up in a fist. "Give her some time."

"Come now, Julius. Into your stall."

Laars returned to the claim in time to put the horse up and check on the cows. He walked through the darkening light to the house.

The stove stood like a cold rebuke and the unwashed dishes mocked him. *Right back where I started—alone, with no help.* Laars opened the oven door and retrieved the last two biscuits from the morning's breakfast that Giovanna had made, *when was it—yesterday?* The trips back and forth to town gave him less time to do his chores and he was dog tired.

Laars lit a lantern and saw Giovanna's and Rosa's bonnets hanging on the hook by the door where she had rushed right past without stopping.

She comes to me with this burden, and expects me to pay and pay. The gloom he felt beget more dark thoughts. *Well, if she thinks she can snooker me into losing my life savings, she has another thing coming!*

Laars took off his boots and tossed them across the floor angrily. With no one to talk to and no energy to read, Laars went into his room and lay down with his arms folded behind his head and his large frame sprawled across the top of the bed. Through the open door across the hall, he could see Giovanna's hairbrush and night cream next to the wash basin.

Achh, is there no end to it? He blew out the lantern to snuff out the view. When his eyes adjusted to the dark, a vision of Giovanna brushing her long, black hair came to him. His mind quieted and he reconciled himself to indulging the image. His last memory before falling asleep was of her looking up and smiling.

Chapter Sixteen

At dawn in her tiny room at the top of the stairs, Giovanna pushed up from the cot and rose stiffly from her knees. Rosa was in God's and Dr. Ledville's hands, and Giovanna could do little now but offer her supplications and tears.

All her years of work to keep Rosa safe, her long trip to Dakota territory, her decision to marry Laars—all of it for nothing if it meant living without Rosa.

She splashed water on her face, and wearily headed down the stairs to the store.

"There she is—dear Giovanna," Mrs. Pavente announced as she appeared in the doorway. "Have you slept at all? You poor thing! Come, have some coffee."

Mrs. Pavente bustled about the kitchen in the back of the store, preparing the days' baked goods for sale and breakfast for her husband and the store helpers.

"I can help you with that," Giovanna said, pointing to the flour-dusted board where Mrs. Pavente was preparing to roll out dough. "I can at least be of some use to you for all your kindness."

"You are more than use to me, you are like a ray of sunshine from the old country, my dear girl," Mrs. Pavente said. "Please, drink up and then yes, you can help as much as you want."

Giovanna spent the morning rolling out biscuits and baking them on large pans in Mrs. Pavente's huge oven. It was the biggest kitchen she had ever seen, and her mind settled as she focused on the familiar work, made easier by the abundance of ingredients and tools at her disposal.

She used a small baking pan to pour batter into 12 long impressions, smiling as she baked the familiar biscotti of her village. When they were done, she arranged them on a tray and brought them to the storefront to put in the display case.

"*Bene, benessima*, Giovanna you have a true talent," Mrs. Pavente said upon sampling the warm treat.

Mr. Pavente unlocked the door to the shop and the first customers of the day trickled in. Giovanna stayed in the kitchen, cleaning and baking, as Mr. and Mrs. Pavente tended to their duties.

"Giovanna, come here!" She heard Mrs. Pavente call. Giovanna dropped her pan and rushed to the front, wiping her hands on her apron.

Mrs. Pavente held a slip of paper toward her. "From Dr. Ledville."

Giovanna reached for the note, but pulled her hand back as if it were the hot stove. "Please, can you read it?"

Mrs. Pavente pursed her lips, opened the page and read:

> *Dear Giovanna,*
>
> *I have word that the hospital is full. Rosa requires treatments that I do not have time to give. Come to her and I will show you what to do.*
>
> *Dr. Ledville*

"Oh no! Mrs. Pavente, I must leave right away!" Giovanna implored her.

"Exactly right. Yes, the boy who brought the note can take you back with him. Giovanni! Finish up with young Jimmy right away!"

Chapter Seventeen

Laars awoke with a stiff neck from a fitful night's sleep. It was light outside already, meaning he had overslept. He searched for his missing boot from where he had tossed them last night, and went to his reading chair to pull it onto his foot.

He sat down on something and pulled Rosa's book out from under his leg. In the light from the window, he traced the intricate letters on the cover.

Opening the pages, he turned to where Rosa had finished.

A small, dried flower held her place in the book. Laars picked it up carefully by its stiff stem in his large fingers. The light from the window shown through the pale lavender petals, and the small bright center retained its full yellow color.

So beautiful, yet so easily broken. Laars looked down at the page and saw something in a small child's hand. He opened the book wider and made out a crudely drawn face of a small cat. The child's letters underneath read, *Pearl*. She had drawn a wobbly heart around the name.

Laars gently replaced the flower in the crease of the book. Closing it, he held the book to his bowed head. Laars Gundersen forgot about the cattle, and his claim, and the dollar amount of his savings. He saw Rosa with Giovanna's arm across her shoulders at the station. He pictured her hiding behind her mother's skirts when they first met his family. He remembered her smiling and laughing with Anna after the wedding.

Then the sound of her piteous coughing filled his ears.

"Rosa." For the first time, he said the child's name out loud as if talking to her. He looked up and thought he could just see them standing there together in the kitchen. What a fool he'd been. Giovanna hadn't brought him an extra burden, just another mouth to feed and someone whose bills he had to pay. She had brought him herself, and her most precious possession: little Rosa. A precious gift if only he had seen it.

Giovanna! He thought of her face and her eyes turning away each time before he could kiss her. She had accepted him and his rough ways and the work to be done without complaint. And he had expected more of her than she could give. No wonder she couldn't love him. He was denying the very truth of her as a woman. She was a mother and loving her child was the key to her loving him.

Father! Mr. Gundersen's words came back to him: *You may go where you want, but you cannot escape yourself.* Before he boarded the train back to Minnesota, he had added: "You left home to start a new life, just as I did so many years ago. You wanted a wife to be the heart of your home, and partner in your efforts. Your responsibility is to love and care for her. Since you have not much practice, expect to have to work as hard at that as you do on the claim."

Laars knew what he had to do. He raced to finish his morning chores, hooked up Julius to the wagon, and took off for town.

Chapter Eighteen

The wagon took several hours to reach Dr. Ledville's house. The road was washed out in places, and Jimmy had to get down and guide the horse around large ruts so the wagon wouldn't tip over.

Please, let the road be clear now! Giovanna thought after each delay. The sun beat down on her uncovered head, causing her to feel faint after her long night without sleep. *I'll be with you soon, my Rosa!*

Dr. Ledville waited as long as he could for Giovanna, then wrote out instructions to leave behind. He checked on Rosa one more time before leaving. *Poor child, if this fever doesn't break tonight, there will be nothing I can do.* Dr. Ledville left the note and the supplies out on the table next to Rosa's bed, closed the door, and set out on his rounds.

Jimmy pulled up to the front of Dr. Ledville's house. He helped Giovanna down from the wagon.

"I'll be back later to check in on you, Mrs. Gundersen," he said. "Have to make these deliveries first; I'm already late with the bad road and all."

"Thank you, Jimmy. I'll be fine now," Giovanna said, and rushed into the quiet house.

The doctor's house featured an entrance hall with a large staircase, two rooms on either side and a long hallway leading to the kitchen. Giovanna looked in each of the rooms.

"Dr. Ledville? Are you home?" Hearing no answer, Giovanna quickly climbed the stairs. She could see the doctor's bedroom door open at the end of the hall, and several other closed doors. She opened them one by one, searching for Rosa. Finally, she opened a door and found her.

Rosa lay under a light coverlet with her dark hair damp and matted against the pillow. The gray light coming through the shaded window cast a ghostly pall over her small features. Giovanna gasped and covered her mouth with her hand. Slowly, she came to the bedside and looked at Rosa, waiting to see her breathe.

Rosa was breathing, slowly, shallowly. Giovanna cried out in relief and hugged her. "My baby, you are still with me! Mama is here now, everything will be all right."

Rosa did not open her eyes even as her mother stroked her cheeks with the back of her hand and gently pulled the hair away from her warm neck. Giovanna took the cloth from the basin next to the bed, squeezed it out, and placed it on Rosa's forehead. She saw a couple of bottles, a mortar and pestle, and piece of paper on the table. She made out the letters "Dr. Ledville" at the bottom, but the rest was incomprehensible to her. Oh, where had he gone and what should she do for Rosa?

I'll be calm and wait here for Jimmy, Giovanna thought. *Let me do the next thing I can do.* She took the basin of lukewarm water and went down to the kitchen to get fresh water from the cold sink.

Chapter Nineteen

*L*aars patted his front pocket as he negotiated the pitted road to Springvale. After he arrived at the Pavente's to find Giovanna gone, he had gone to the bank and withdrawn the money needed for the hospital. *If they see I can pay, they will surely take her.*

The sun hung low in the sky as he pulled up to Dr. Ledville's house. He climbed the porch steps in the gloom to knock at the door without benefit of light from any window.

Giovanna sat on the chair next to Rosa, her head down on her arms on the bed. *Bam-bam-bam. Bam-bam-bam.* The sound of knocking gradually broke through to her consciousness. *Jimmy! He must be back!*

Rushing down the stairs, Giovanna threw open the door and reached forward with one hand to pull Jimmy quickly in after her. Laars stood with his hand in mid-air from knocking and he quickly grasped her by the wrist.

"Laars! It's you! I was expecting—oh never mind!" Her red-rimmed eyes looked up at him as her free hand rose to the sky in desperation. "Please, come quickly!"

Wanting to pull her to him, Laars instead released her arm and followed her inside.

"What can I do?" Laars said.

Quickly they went to Rosa's room and retrieved the supplies and note Dr. Ledville had left. Laars took one look at Rosa and shook his head sadly. *Surely, we are too late.*

Giovanna insisted he come to the kitchen and read her the instructions while she prepared the treatment.

Laars read, "Make a strong tea of the willow bark inside the blue jar. Give her full strength the first hour, and half strength every hour after that." He paused, as if to ask a question before continuing. "If you can get enough in her and if she can keep it down, it may break the fever. If not, she will be in God's hands."

Giovanna shredded the bark into smaller pieces while Laars brought in wood for the stove. He lit the fire for her, filled the heavy kettle with water, and lifted it to the stove. Laars was happy to help, but puzzled why Giovanna had waited so long to carry out Dr. Ledville's direction.

As the fire sparked hotter, Giovanna stood waiting for it to boil.

"You know what they say about a watched pot, Giovanna," Laars said gently. "Come sit down while the water heats. I have something to ask you."

Giovanna's eyes stayed glued to the kettle. "What is it?"

"Can you read Dr. Ledville's note to me?"

Chapter Twenty

"Oh, Laars!" Giovanna said, turning from the stove and putting her hands at rest on the table.

He quietly pulled a chair out and took her by the elbow to help her sit.

"There is no shame in it," Laars said.

"The letter I wrote to you—well, I cannot yet write in English. Or read. I didn't write the letter."

"But it was about you, how you look, what you can do—it's exactly right," Laars said. "Well—everything except the truth about Rosa."

"Yes. My good friend, Mrs. Forsythe, brought me your ad. She wrote the letter for me as I spoke. I thought she was writing everything I said. I talked of myself, yes, but also about Rosa; that she was sick, and needed a doctor. I had so many worries.

"Jo, I didn't know," Laars said.

"I'm sure she was just trying to make me seem more—acceptable—to you."

Laars considered her words. In a few days' time, she had already made his house a home with her loving presence.

Her heart that so loved her daughter—this was the heart he wanted to love him. If he could even share just a bit of the love she had, he could be a happy man.

"Is that why you cried all night your first night here? You were worried about Rosa?" Laars asked. "Why didn't you say anything?"

"Yes, I mean, no—" Giovanna faltered. She had first compromised her honesty by allowing Mrs. Forsythe to lie about her age. Then Mrs. Forsythe had complicated everything by not writing about her worries for Rosa in her first letter. It was time to stop hiding even small things from Laars, as they had a way of making bigger problems. She had not been married long enough the first time to learn the truth of this, but she felt it with all her heart now.

"When I first arrived, I worried that you had not told me the truth. I let my fears overwhelm what my eyes could see. I was afraid I had made a mistake in coming here. And I found instead, that you didn't know the whole truth about me. I'm sorry, Laars. I will understand if you decide that you cannot continue this marriage of false pretenses."

"Jo—" Laars began, but no more words would come. His mind was filled with the sight of her beautiful face, its forehead smooth and eyebrows straight with no trace of guile or malice, her wide, perfect lips held parted but with no hint of a smile. And mostly, his heart was pierced by the determined look in her eyes. She was offering him to cut his losses, and in exchange giving all of herself to the plight of her child.

"I can't," he said.

Giovanna's eyes twitched in a

moment of disbelief, before hardening slightly.

"I understand."

The kettle began to whistle and Giovanna rose to pour the hot water into a bowl to steep the willow bark.

"No, Jo. I can't let you go," Laars said. "I love you."

Her eyelashes fluttered and her chin dropped, parting her beautiful lips into the hint of a smile. Could this be true?

Before she could turn away, Laars leaned down and planted a warm, gentle kiss on her lips. She let her arms reach around him as he pulled her in close. Giovanna didn't think, didn't stop him, didn't do anything; she just received the love Laars offered.

In her quiet surrender, Laars felt his heart nearly burst from its chest. "You're my wife, Jo," he whispered. "Let me do some of the worrying now. We'll get through this together."

Chapter Twenty-one

 iovanna carefully lifted Rosa's head and blew on the surface of the cup to cool the tea. "Come dear, take another sip," she said.

The warm tea dribbled a bit out of Rosa's mouth before she was roused enough to part her lips and swallow. Laars stood at the end of the bed, gripping the iron frame with both hands as he watched for any sign of improvement.

"There, that's the third cup," Giovanna said.

"What do we do now?" Laars asked, hating the feeling of uselessness that engulfed him.

Footsteps sounded outside the door. "We wait," Dr. Ledville said. He crossed the room, felt Rosa's cheeks, and bent over and listened to her heart.

"Doctor, I must speak with you!" Laars said, beckoning him outside the room.

Laars closed the door behind them. "Dr. Ledville, you must arrange for Rosa's placement at the hospital tomorrow. I can pay cash," he said, patting the bulge in his front shirt pocket.

"That's fine, Mr. Gundersen, mighty fine. Only it won't help." Dr. Ledville said. "The hospital is plum full up, what with consumption and chickenpox all around these parts. I couldn't get her in if you gave me a thousand dollars!"

"Who's going to give you a thousand dollars?" asked Giovanna, standing in the open doorway and looking at Dr. Ledville. Her eyes followed his to Laars's face. She noticed his hand at his chest and he smiled sheepishly at her.

"Laars! I thought we couldn't afford to—I was going to pay for it—Mrs. Pavente can give me work..." Giovanna started.

"Looks like you have a fine man to take care of you, Giovanna," Dr. Ledville said. "Truth be told, I don't think the hospital is the best place for her now even if it had room. I've seen a lot of cases of consumption, but this isn't like that. No, the little girl has scarlet fever in my opinion. The cure will come when her fever breaks. Until then, her body is fighting the poison of the illness."

"Not consumption?" Giovanna said hopefully. Her deepest fear, that Rosa would succumb as Frank had, began to recede. "But this fever, what if it doesn't come down?"

"She's fought it a long time and her body is weak. If her temperature stays this high for too much longer...." His voice trailed off, unable to speak the words to Giovanna's distraught face. "It's been a long day. Come and wake me if anything changes. I'll check in with you at first light."

Giovanna stood stricken in the doorway with the water basin in her hand. "I was just going to get more cold water," she said.

"Here, let me do that," Laars said. His large hand covered hers and she transferred the weight of the basin to him.

Giovanna looked into his beautiful blue eyes and felt them smiling right into her soul. He blinked slowly and his lips parted into a shy grin. In all her conversations with him, Giovanna Gundersen didn't know if she ever really took full account of her husband. His straight, broad nose was framed by wide cheeks and lines that crinkled when he smiled. His broad shoulders moved easily inside his thin cotton shirt. He would take care of her. He had said it, and he meant it.

Chapter Twenty-two

Giovanna and Laars sat up all night in chairs across the bed from Rosa. Between ministrations of tea and replacing cold cloths, they shared the effort to finally relieve her of the fever. They talked quietly and even smiled a time or two. Giovanna at one point fell asleep with her head leaned back in the chair.

Laars took the chance to admire her without her seeing. He longed to hold her but knew now it would depend on whether Rosa came through. He had proven his love, but it was still too late. If Rosa dies, Giovanna may never forgive me for the delay, he thought. He despaired at the prospect of losing them both.

The first ray of sunlight turned the inky blackness to a dark purple, and soon the sky would lighten to a violet, then dark blue before the sun blazed over another light blue sky. Rosa stirred under the covers and Laars stood next to her to see whether he should wake Giovanna.

He watched her face twitch and her small tongue came out to wet her lips. He put his hand to her forehead and her lashes fluttered open.

"P-papa?" She said. The hoarse whisper barely broke the silence. *Papa*.

"Yes, Rosa, I'm your Papa now," Laars whispered.

"Where's Mama? I'm hungry," Rosa said.

"She's right here, asleep by your side."

"I was having the strangest dream," Rosa said, her dark eyes looking earnestly straight into Laars's blue ones. He had never seen such an old soul peering at him from such a young child's face.

"I was dreaming about Pearl," Rosa said. "She was mewing and meowing for me, and I couldn't find her!"

"I'm sure Pearl's all right," Laars said. "You must have been dreaming about the new litter of kittens I found in the barn yesterday. I've been waiting for you to get better to come home and take care of them. I thought you might like two I picked out for you, a gray one and a white calico."

"Two kittens? Oh, Papa, can I see them now?"

Laars laughed and woke Giovanna with a start, as his deep chuckle broke the gloom of the recent days' tension and fear.

"Laars, what—? Rosa? Are you awake?" Giovanna said as she rose to her feet.

She placed her hands on the child's face and looked into her fully awake dark eyes and pale face. Laars held his breath until he saw the smile of joy spreading across Giovanna's face.

"Laars, the fever has broken! My Rosa is coming back to me!"

"Our Rosa, my sweet Jo," Laars said.

He placed his hand on Giovanna's back and reached over her to smooth a piece of Rosa's hair. "If you'll share her with me."

Giovanna felt her heart would burst at the words. "Gladly, my dear Laars," she said. "With all my heart."

THE END

About the Author

*L*orena Dove has been reading and dreaming about living during the great westward migration since she was a young child growing up in New York and then Virginia. A descendent of Italian and German immigrants, she enjoys the interplay of cultures and passing down of traditions, recipes and family values to her children and grandchildren.

Lorena raised four children in a modernized 1880s log cabin for 10 years in West Virginia. The seasons of nature, the beauty of the mountains and rivers, and the simple enjoyment of gardening, reading and quilting have been her passions.

She now lives with her husband, a retired Marine Corps colonel, and sons in Virginia. She collaborates on books with her daughter, whose passion for historical fiction exceeds her own, and is waiting for her grand-daughters to fit into their mother's dress-up hoopskirts and bonnets.

You can keep in touch with Lorena by visiting her Facebook page at Lorena Dove Books, or sign up for her VIP Readers Group at www.LorenaDove.com.

More Books in the Sweet Land of Liberty Brides Series

Book 2 – Nathalie: *The Circuit Rider's Rhineland Mail Order Bride* ~ Can practical Nathalie find love in the strong arms of an intellectual dreamer?

Book 3: Silvia: *The Stockman's Slovak Mail Order Bride* ~ Silvia flees a turbulent past for the west, hoping for safety and dreaming of love. Can Dell, a 'Black Irish' stockman and reformed fighter, win her heart if he must fight for it?

Also by Lorena Dove

Mail Order Bride: Saved by Grace

Fraternal twins, Annabelle and Willie, whose widowed father is about to marry a woman that hates them, send for a mail-order bride.

Mail Order Bride: Celia's Secret Baby

Abandoned as a child, Celia determines to carry on with her plan to be a mail order bride even after the death of her best friend at the orphanage.

Mail Order Bride: Angie's Hope

Angie is ready for her engagement to expire when she meets and falls in love with Cal.

Christmas Bride: Susan's Secret Baby

A widow with a secret heads to the Oklahoma Territories as a possible wife for a lonely farmer with three children.

Find these and all new releases by
Lorena Dove on Amazon, or visit

http://www.LorenaDove.com

http://www.Facebook.com/LorenaDoveBooks